AF353093

RANGE

ANDREW DAVIE

Copyright (C) 2022 Andrew Davie

Layout design and Copyright (C) 2022 by Next Chapter

Published 2022 by Next Chapter

Edited by Charity Rabbiosi

Cover art by Michaela Jacinto

Mass Market Paperback Edition

This book is a work of fiction. Names, characters, places, and incidents are the product of the author's imagination or are used fictitiously. Any resemblance to actual events, locales, or persons, living or dead, is purely coincidental.

All rights reserved. No part of this book may be reproduced or transmitted in any form or by any means, electronic or mechanical, including photocopying, recording, or by any information storage and retrieval system, without the author's permission.

For Owen and Simon

ACKNOWLEDGMENTS

Thank you, Heather and Jan for reading earlier drafts and providing feedback. Thank you, Bryant for the story about cuisine, and Chris for the copyedits. Thank you, Miika and the Next Chapter team.

THE PLANE BANKED WITH THE TURBULENCE, and almost everyone on the flight grabbed their arm rests. The exceptions included a few soldiers Lawson could only imagine were pilots who'd seen much worse up close. They weren't even phased. The other soldiers who hadn't reacted may have previously been considered for section eights and would never be able to adjust to life back in the world.

"Get you somethin, hon?" the stewardess said.

Lawson looked over. She was standing in the aisle directly next to him. He hadn't even heard her approach. If he'd still been in the jungle, he would have been dead.

"Coke, please."

She filled a cup with ice and popped the top off a bottle. She had blonde hair, green eyes, and very angular features. She wouldn't have been a pin up girl, but she was attractive. More importantly, she was the first American girl Lawson had seen in months. Up close, the bright colors of her uniform bordered on overpowering. Still, though.

"I'm Lawson," he began to say then added, "Herb."

"Cheryl. Nice to meet you."

She handed him the coke. Her smile was something else. Lawson didn't believe there was a real connection; he knew she genuinely cared about the boys coming back home, and her kindness hadn't been forced. He also knew she would smile like that at everyone who spoke with her. He laughed. it would take him a while to get used to saying *Herb* again.

He watched Cheryl move further down the aisle and took a sip of his drink.

It felt like only yesterday he was short twenty days

and going out on his final patrol before his team leader, Matthew Rainwood, who said Lawson would be put on administrative duties. They may have needed every able body in the field, but Rainwood looked out for his guys especially if they were that short.

Lawson drank more of his soda, pinched the bridge of his nose, and shut his eyes. He had allowed himself time before he left to process everything. He knew if he thought about it again he'd lose it, and that was the last thing he needed, to lose it during the fourth hour of a fifteen hour flight. Lawson managed to white knuckle through the desire to contemplate the uncertainty of his future, and instead focused on his final patrol.

The team had been just within the cover of the jungle, but they had a clear view of the bridge and road. Intel had come down that the bridge was being used for enemy activity and needed to be leveled. The squad was going to assess the situation and quarterback an air strike.

"Toss it," Rainwood had said.

As their team leader, Rainwood had been responsible for everything. He took care of the recon team, and even though he was roughly the same age, he'd become a father figure to most of them. A member of the Mashantucket Pequot tribe, he took pride in his heritage, though he'd had to keep a standard military style haircut, forgoing his usual style which hung down to his ribs.

Sal Raskavanitch, the assistant radio operator had the best arm, so he would throw the smoke. Raskavanitch was from some Midwest town outside of Chicago. He said he'd been scouted by some colleges to play center field. No one believed it until one day, while filling sandbags, he launched a stone into the jungle. They didn't know how far it had gone but was enough to confirm he'd probably been telling the truth.

"I got three to one it gets caught in the branches," Lawson said. He was the point man from New York City: Hell's Kitchen. A degenerate gambler, he'd bet on everything, but he kept things light and was as solid as they came.

Raskavanitch threw the smoke cannister which cleared the trees and landed exactly where it was supposed to.

"Damn," Lawson said after the throw. "I guess they really know how to grow 'em in Pea Pod," he added.

"Paw Paw," Raskavanitch said.

Within a moment, the cannister begin emitting a thick cloud of purple smoke.

"Echo Tango this is Alpha Foxtrot, we've popped smoke," Jeremiah Jackson, the radio operator said. Jackson had black square frame glasses which made his eyes look twice their normal size. He was given to most superstitions imaginable, and before every patrol, went through a ritual that ended with him kissing the crucifix he wore around his neck.

The Forward Air Controller had already given them their options of aircraft in the vicinity, and soon an F4 would arrive and Napalm the area.

"Alpha Foxtrot, I have purple smoke, over," the FAC replied.

"Roger that, Alpha Foxtrot out."

The FAC suggested all groups within a few hundred yards button up since the F4 would go to work with 40-mike-mike and nape the area.

"Were there any takers on the arm from Pea Pod?" Lawson said.

"Herb," Rainwood said. His tone wasn't angry, but it was stern. Lawson gave it a rest. The F4 made its pass, the explosions shook the ground, and lit up the vicinity even though it was still daytime. No matter how many times Lawson smelled Napalm, he still retched. He wasn't nauseated, but there was something about the smell that disagreed with him. When he'd first arrived, he'd carried some tablets, but they didn't do anything. In the end, he realized it was just another thing he'd have to endure, like the time he was on R and R in Japan and discovered they put mayonnaise on pizza, and it would be almost impossible to get it without.

Dom Garibaldi, the assistant team leader, rarely spoke. Even during a skirmish, he had a quiet stoic quality. He got Rainwood's attention and made a motion with his hand accounting for everyone. It wasn't necessary since all of them had been present, but Garibaldi followed procedure regardless.

"Take your positions," Rainwood said, and they began to move. They would survey the damage wrought by the F4. Most of the time, there wasn't much left to examine. It was nasty stuff. Lawson always found it perplexing and the smell would make him feel sick, but he didn't have a problem with discovering charred remains.

The plane banked again and brought him out of his memory. He realized he'd been sweating and gripping both of his armrests. He finished the rest of his soda. He was about to ring Cheryl to get another but figured he'd just ask her on her way back.

Lawson tried to think of more pleasant things.

When he got home, he'd have some catching up to do celebrating the Knicks championship he'd missed. He'd made a killing on their victory. He was able to get great odds after they lost the first game. The final game was played in Los Angeles and kicked off at 1930 which made it 0930 where they were. Lawson knew he'd catch hell but made sure to get out of whatever duty he'd been assigned in order to listen to the broadcast. Lawson smiled at the memory. He wouldn't have a sizable bankroll when he got home, but it would be enough to get started. He wondered if Elmo was still taking book, but even if he wasn't, Lawson would find someone else. A pang in his stomach made him realize that as much as he was trying to fight it, he'd return to thinking about the last mission.

William "Billy" O'Sullivan had been the *slack man*, the team's pack animal. Still a cherry, he was a good kid from some small town on the Florida panhandle. He was always asking questions, but since they were a small unit, they all looked at him like a little brother who needed help. Rather than shut him out they did the opposite. They still busted his chops, though.

After surveying the carnage from the F4, the team was on their way back to camp. Lawson had been in the front leading the way, followed by the rest of them. O'-Sullivan was fifth in the order with Garibaldi taking the rear. O'Sullivan was thin before he'd got in country, but he'd lost enough weight to make him gaunt and sunken — probably getting a parasite at some point. His clothes hung off of him. He looked more like a kid playing soldier with his friends. Lawson heard the sound of the explosion followed by the screaming. O'-Sullivan had stepped on a *Mosquito Mine*, the VC version of the toe popper. It was the empty shell of a large caliber bullet packed with gunpowder and some debris. The shell was placed in bamboo sleeve with a nail at the bottom and wax on top. They weren't designed to kill, just maim to slow things down. Most soldiers who triggered them might lose a toe or a part of their foot. O'Sullivan had the misfortune to step on one that sent shrapnel into his inner thigh and nicked his femoral artery.

He bled out before they could get him back.

The memory dissipated, and Lawson opened his

eyes. He'd been crying, but thankfully it was silent. He wiped his eyes.

Cheryl didn't have the cart with her the next time she passed by, but she said she'd bring him another coke, and he could keep the bottle.

Brennan's pub had peanut shells on the floor. Lawson didn't know if that had been a conscious decision. Since every table had a bowl full of peanuts, maybe it just made sense to the owner to incorporate it into the decor. It would have been impossible to keep the place clean otherwise.

The fact the bar was dimly lit also helped.

Eventually, the feel and sound of shells crunching on the floor became second nature.

Brennan's had one countertop to the right with a couple of taps and a few spaced out bowls of peanuts. They had spirits behind the bar, but people hardly ever ordered them. There was a jukebox, but it only played one record: "In The Wee Small Hours" by Frank Sinatra. The machine housed other records, but that was the only one which was accessible.

The bar truly catered to only one client: Randall Fitzpatrick. Those in Fitzpatrick's crew, and some locals, understood the rules. So, they ordered their draughts, ate peanuts, and listened to Frank Sinatra croon. Fitzpatrick wasn't a heavyweight in his own right. He still deferred to the major players who ran the city, but he was certainly someone who had to be taken seriously. He'd set up shop in Hell's Kitchen, and though he and his crew dabbled in a few different enterprises, it was bookmaking and loansharking which were his bread and butter. Once Lawson returned, he wasted almost no time making up for his absence from the scene. Elmo had gone, but there were other games in town. Lawson went in deep on college and the pros, and it wasn't long before he was one of Fitzpatrick's regulars.

Fitzpatrick was at his table with Ridley, who kept the book, and Horst, who collected. Aside from loving the music, Fitzpatrick had also fashioned himself after Sinatra: the clothes, hairstyle, and even kept a roll of dimes in his pocket after he'd learned Sinatra did the same. When Lawson had asked Fitzpatrick about the dimes, the others in the vicinity had rolled their eyes. Their eyeroll wasn't obvious. No one would have disrespected Fitzpatrick openly, but they must have heard the story incessantly. Apparently, while Sinatra had been filming *Robin and the 7 Hoods*, his son, Frank Jr, had been kidnapped. The kidnappers had demanded all communication be done over payphone, so the elder Sinatra always made sure to carry ten dimes.

Lawson walked through the bar toward the table with the three of them. He sat down, placed an envelope on the table, and slid it toward Ridley who took it and quickly thumbed through to make sure it was all there. Ridley had a button-down shirt and suspenders. He looked like he should be helping someone with their tax return rather than keeping book for Fitzpatrick. Ridley produced a moleskin notebook and pencil and made a few quick notations.

"The Knickerbockers ain't what they used to be," Fitzpatrick said.

Lawson nodded in agreement.

"You starting to take action on NCAA?" Lawson said.

Ridley consulted his book.

"UCLA's a lock," Horst said.

Horst took a swig of his beer. His nose had been busted, probably a few times, and had never been fixed.

It made his face seem like everything was out of alignment. He also kept his chin down, so he looked at you from the tops of his eyes. He was being conservative by suggesting UCLA would win. They were the logical choice. UCLA had won seven titles in a row and another two before that to win nine titles in ten years.

"Except Kareem's not there anymore, and they peaked in the finals last year," Lawson said.

Horst stared at him.

"Not to mention, this year they lost to Notre Dame, Oregon, and Oregon St."

"Rid," Horst said and looked over to Ridley who was busy thumbing through his notebook. Ridley didn't look up; he could multitask though, so it wasn't an insult.

"Yeah?"

"What's the line on UCLA?"

"It's not out yet, but they're heavy favorites."

No one spoke for another moment, then Horst addressed Lawson.

"It's going to be eight in a row."

"OK."

Lawson had never discovered if Horst was his first or last name. Horst didn't look like much. He was only five-five, but Lawson had seen him go to work on people who'd been twice his size. Horst possessed a ferocity Lawson had never seen in people before, just wild animals. Lawson thought to ask whether Horst had been checked for rabies, but he didn't want to give the man any excuses to start things. If Horst ever got the green light from Fitzpatrick, it would be trouble.

"Gimme two hundred on NC State," Lawson said.

Ridley looked to Fitzpatrick who opened his eyes and nodded. Ridley wrote it in the book.

"I'll be around," sang Sinatra from the jukebox. It had an ominous sound to it.

Lawson had found a job as an apprentice at a shop in the Diamond District. Seymour Hershfeld, the shop owner, had married outside of his community. Essentially, he'd been shunned, but he continued to be observant. Little changed except the people with whom Seymour socialized. He'd made his decision though, and while it was difficult at times, he said he had never regretted it.

When Seymour's brother-in-law's son, Herb, needed a job, Seymour gave him one. Lawson had aptitude for the position. Within a few years, he'd be able to start work as a bench jeweler. Seymour was always at the store when Lawson got there in the morning, and he was still there when Lawson left. Not that Lawson had the same enthusiasm for the minerals that Seymour did, but Lawson had taken to the job nonetheless.

"How's the ring for Mrs. Titlebaum?" Seymour said once Lawson had sat down at his workstation.

"2 p.m.," Lawson said.

"Good work, boychik," Seymour replied. He wore traditional Hasidic clothes: long suit, black hat, and gartel. The tallit was removed once he got to the shop. When it was the winter, he wore a shtreimel. He would often bring food from home and eat at his desk. Seymour placed a hand on Lawson's shoulder and squeezed. Though he had a thick grey beard, it was easy to tell when he smiled. Seymour walked away to greet the others who were busy trickling in at the start of the day. Seymour would greet each of them individually, probably discuss the time Walt Frasier had come in a little while ago to get some custom rings, and eventually Seymour would take his place behind the counter in the front.

Lawson went back to work. Most of his day-to-day responsibilities had to do with helping to load and unload merchandise, sweep up the store, set things up, but he was learning. He had begun to be trusted with finishing up the polishing on a few pieces, and he was learning how to set stones.

Regardless, it was better than running point for the Recon team. At least this way, he didn't have to worry about someone trying to kill him. As long as he kept Horst from showing up unexpectedly to collect. He could do that. He believed in the law of averages, and UCLA's run was due to end at some point. Most of the work on Mrs. Titlebaum's ring had been done already, but Lawson finished buffing and boxing it. He left it with Seymour at the front, checked the time, and grabbed his coat to head for lunch.

1974

Lawson finished setting the gem in the pendant and put the needle nose pliers on the table. He sat back and rolled his head to loosen his neck. He would always tighten up when he was setting stones. For whatever reason, since his final tour, he would tense up when he had to focus intently. He'd tried a ton of different methods to remain calm, but none of them had any success.

He examined his work and placed it on a towel in his drawer before he shut and locked it. He could finish it after lunch. Lawson grabbed his coat, cap, and gloves from the coat rack. It was only the beginning of September, but they'd already experienced a bit of a cold spell. On the way to the front, he stopped by Seymour's office. The man was busy looking over papers that had been spread out across his desk.

"You want anything?" Lawson said. He knew Seymour would refuse, but he never stopped offering.

"No, thanks," Seymour said.

"You sure? They got great blintzes."

Lawson didn't wait for Seymour to reiterate his answer. It was the same routine everyday including the conversation about blintzes. However, today would be different. Rainwood had called the previous evening, said he was in town, and asked for Lawson to meet him. The first year after Lawson had been discharged, they had done a better job keeping in touch, but it had been a while. Then last night, the phone rang, and it was Rainwood. They caught up for a few minutes before Rainwood had asked if they could meet up. Lawson suggested the diner near work and told Rainwood he'd get an hour for lunch. Rainwood said that would be fine. There had been a strange tone to Rainwood's voice, but Lawson didn't bring it up.

In country, Rainwood had always kept his hair in a crew cut. Before certain excursions, he would fashion it into a mohawk. Now it was to his shoulders. He looked the same as Lawson had remembered, but now there was a skittish quality to him, and he lacked the confidence he once had.

"I'll level with you, Herb," Rainwood said and stated he had returned home to a lot of upheaval. Earlier this year, the Indian Affairs Council had been created to oversee governance of their own land as well as the removal of certain restrictions. However, it was still bleak. The American Indian Movement had had a standoff with the FBI in Pine Ridge which left a few dead and reinforced an already existing antagonism toward Native Americans.

In Vietnam, Rainwood was a capable leader of a team of six, responsible for keeping his group alive. Back home, there were few options— except getting loaded every day and living off a government stipend.

"I need to feel it again," Rainwood said. "Or, I'm going to spiral out."

Lawson didn't have any answers, but he knew what Rainwood had been talking about. Lawson knew he'd been lucky to get the gig working for Seymour who probably wouldn't have hired him if there hadn't been a family connection.

"What are you thinking?" Lawson said.

Rainwood took out a magazine, *Soldier of Fortune*. He opened it to a dogeared page, turned the magazine upside-down, and slid it toward Lawson.

The article was about the current skirmish in Rhodesia.

"Africa?" Lawson said. He took a sip of his coffee. Rainwood smiled, sat back in his chair, and took another sip of his drink. The waitress came by.

"You fellas good?"

"Sure, thanks, Donna," Lawson said.

Lawson had been going to the diner almost every day for lunch; he'd become familiar with most of the staff.

"Just let me know," she said and went to take another order.

Rainwood sat forward.

"Ranchers," he began. "Cattle rustling has become a problem."

He'd underlined some of the important information. There was also a map and he'd circled some of the areas in Rhodesia and Mozambique.

"We'd be range detectives like the old Pinkertons."

Rainwood's trademark smirk appeared like when he'd outlined a solid plan for the team to follow.

Lawson continued to read. Cattle were a main export of the white minority government, so rustling was a way for the guerrillas to deal a serious blow. The military and police had been tasked with combat on the front lines, so the ranchers were hiring mercenaries. The first few hires had been adequate, but couldn't stem the tide, so the ranchers upped their asking prices and began soliciting candidates with war-time experience. The pay was seven Rhodesian dollars a day, and a seven hundred-fifty bonus for each rustler apprehended.

"I'm not interested in the politics or the pay," Rainwood said. He had read the look on Lawson's face, took a final drink of his beer, and spoke again.

"Before you say no."

To buy some more time, Lawson asked Rainwood whether he'd heard from anyone else on the team. Lawson had been lousy at keeping in contact with everyone. Except for Rainwood who had previously contacted Lawson, Jackson was the only one who Lawson knew about. Jackson had gotten strung out, and last Lawson heard, Jackson had been busted buying from an undercover police officer. He was awaiting trial, but it didn't look good.

"What about Raskavanitch?" Lawson said.

"Dropped off the map, spoke to his mother. They hadn't heard from him in months."

"In Pea Pod?"

Lawson had tried to lighten the mood, but Rainwood hadn't played along.

"Yes."

"What about Garibaldi?"

"Got a wife, kids, job as a middle school teacher."

"Alright." Lawson took another sip of his coffee. "When do we leave?"

Lawson hadn't missed the action, but he owed Rainwood. The man had saved his life both literally and metaphorically. If this was the way for Lawson to settle his tab, then so be it. It was going to be difficult to tell Seymour, but it had to be done. Lawson's room had been paid out for the year, and he didn't have any other responsibilities.

Lawson returned to work as soon as he said goodbye to Rainwood. They made plans to rendezvous in a few days; Rainwood would take care of all of the details, contact the fixer who would set them up, and make the transportation arrangements. Lawson would wait until the end of the day to break the news to Seymour. Hopefully, it had been a good day and Seymour would take the news well. Regardless, it wasn't something Lawson had been looking forward to doing. When it was a half an hour after everyone had already left the office, Lawson was still at his workstation. Lawson had done some unpleasant things in his day, so why was this giving him so much trouble?

"Don't burn the candle at both ends, boychik," Seymour said. He was standing a few feet away with the keys to the store in his hand ready to lock up.

"I need to speak with you," Lawson as able to finally say, but it came out as a whisper.

"Excuse me?"

"I need to speak with you," Lawson said again. This time he spoke at his normal register.

"What about?"

Lawson was about to ask if they could adjourn to Seymour's office in the back, but Lawson figured this was as good a place as any. He revealed some of the details of his tour with the Recon team and talked about some of the difficult things he'd had to do; Rainwood had saved his life more than once, and he owed Rainwood a debt. Since Rainwood had asked for backup with his newest venture in Africa, it was the least Lawson could do. Seymour didn't speak the whole time. When Lawson finished, Seymour finally spoke.

"Come with me."

Lawson followed Seymour back into his office. Seymour turned on the overhead light. Lawson had only been in Seymour's office a handful of times. It was sparsely decorated in subtle tones. Seymour opened the top drawer of his desk, removed a bottle of Glenrothes Bourbon Cask Reserve and two glasses. He had noticed Lawson's look of surprise.

"Don't worry, it's Kosher," Seymour said.

Seymour opened the bottle, which had been about half full, and poured both of them two fingers worth. He handed Lawson his glass.

"You have my blessing," Seymour said.

They clinked glasses and each drank. Seymour placed his glass on the desk next to a family picture including his wife and their children. Seymour stared at it for a moment before he spoke.

"Do what you have to do," Seymour said. "The job is waiting for you when you return."

"Thank you."

They finished their drinks.

Seymour put the bottle back in the drawer and wiped the glasses with a rag.

"Well, Boychick," Seymour began. "I guess this is farewell until you return."

Lawson felt overcome with emotion. None of this was playing out the way he had envisioned, but he was relieved.

"Thank you," Lawson said. It was all he could get out.

Seymour put on his coat. "Don't forget to lock up

when you leave." He lingered for a moment longer then left the office.

———

Within seventy-two hours, Rainwood and Lawson were at a ranch in Mazunga, Rhodesia. The fixer with whom Rainwood negotiated had come through with transportation and weapons. Henri, the fixer, had fought in The Algerian War. When it ended, he decided to stay in Africa and moved to Zaire. There were plenty of opportunities to provide arms and services. Henri also had a pretty reliable network through most of the neighboring countries.

Since his conversation with Rainwood in the diner, Lawson had familiarized himself with the history of the area specifically with the last few years of the Bush War. Most of the combat would be taking place on the front, but Rainwood and Lawson would be prepared if things got hairy and the geography of the war changed. In the meantime, they would protect the ranch and stop rustling, which had become an effective irregular tactic.

Both of them would patrol the surrounding area and secure the ranch. They hadn't openly discussed the rules of engagement, but Lawson understood they weren't abiding by any lawful edicts. Currently, both Lawson and Rainwood sat on the porch that overlooked a vast expanse of land.

They drank iced tea with the family and went over various different scenarios of how the family should respond if they were attacked. Three of the five family members sat at rapt attention: Amy, John, and Kelly.

Amy was a British ex-patriate who'd come to Rhodesia about twenty years previously. She reminded Lawson of a settler: plain, but strong and capable. She had married John, who was also a British ex-pat but had grown up in Rhodesia and worked on the ranch which he now owned. He was a barrel-chested man with sideburns and sun-bleached blonde hair.

The family had a few people who worked part time on the farm, but it was a small enough operation. Earlier, they had met Walenti, the Ranch foreman and caretaker. He was a softspoken man and not overtly muscular, but John suggested Walenti was the strongest man he had ever met.

As Lawson had discovered about most things in life, the reality of the situation was more complex than he'd anticipated. While the one side was primarily composed of the white minority government and their supporters, it would also include Black Africans. John and his family didn't seem overtly political, and they clearly didn't believe in a racial hierarchy since they had happily employed Walenti.

Kelly, the family's middle child, was about fifteen and wore a floral print dress. She sat ramrod straight in the wooden chair. She had been enamored with the idea of English aristocracy and now tried to emulate it.

"So, we need to have an escape plan. Where's a place that's easy to get from here?" Rainwood asked. He surveyed the faces of his audience and noted the fear. "Only as a last resort, if things go really bad," he added.

Rainwood smiled, and they relaxed. Christopher, the youngest son at six, was sitting down on the porch coloring in a book. Thomas, the eldest of the children at seventeen, wore overalls and was barefooted. He held a Winchester lever action repeating rifle and kept scanning the horizon as he listened to Rainwood. He looked a little like a younger version of his father. All of the family had been courteous and hospitable to their guests and paid attention to the instructions that were issued. Thomas had been the most willing to help, and both Rainwood and Lawson made sure to include the boy to make him feel as though he was an integral part of the team. In reality though, he would be kept out of harm's way.

"How about the Mtetengwe?" Thomas said and looked to his parents.

"It's a river just south of here," John said. "There are two dams."

"How far?" Rainwood asked.

"About thirty kilometers," Thomas said.

Rainwood paused for a moment and digested the information.

"What transportation do you have?"

"A station wagon, a tractor, and a dirt bike," John said. "Oh, and the farm truck."

"Alright, John and Amy will take Kelly and Christopher in the station wagon."

Rainwood paused a moment.

"Thomas?"

"Yes, sir."

"You think you can manage the bike?"

"Absolutely, sir."

"OK. We'll try to give you enough of a warning, and if things go rotten, we'll rendezvous at the Mtetengue."

"Will it come to that?" Amy asked.

"Doubtful," Lawson said. He hadn't spoken the whole time, but he could sense the dread and wanted to provide a little reassurance. Amy nodded.

"We still have to cover it," Lawson said.

Both he and Rainwood had been able to get all of what they needed from Henri along with a cache of weapons. However, it was just as important to go over contingency plans with the family.

Rainwood looked at the notepad on his lap.

"Last thing; a lock box."

Rainwood didn't wait for questions, and he immediately explained if any of them had valuables they couldn't part with, they would put them in the lock box and bury it in a location nearby. Once things had settled down, or the family had decided to leave, they could retrieve their valuables.

"Think about it," Rainwood said. "Let's meet back here in half an hour."

Slowly, the family dispersed, all except for Christopher, still enamored with his book, who had to be called inside. Lawson and Rainwood were left on the porch. They finished their glasses of iced tea and walked the perimeter. Both men dealt with some of the effects of jetlag, but it hadn't taken long for both of them to shake some of the rust. Within another day, Lawson figured both of them would be sharp enough to patrol the area at full capacity. There'd be only two of them, so they would need to make a few adjustments.

Thomas had already offered to join them, and Rainwood said they needed him to stay in the house to protect his family. The boy had accepted that and taken it as a point of pride he was being trusted with his family's wellbeing. Of course, the truth was that he would have simply gotten in the way out in the bush, and they couldn't risk it.

While the ranch looked similar to many Lawson had seen in photos from farms in the Midwest, the backdrop was breathtaking. He still hadn't gotten used to the fact that wild animals would be lurking in the distance, and in some directions there was nothing but plains.

Both men had decided to bivouac near the cattle pen. The family had offered them room in the main house, but both declined as it would be easier to be closer to the target. They returned to the house forty minutes after finishing their perimeter scouting, and the family members had gathered in the dining room.

Each of them sat with their items of value in front of them.

Lawson laid a duffle bag out on the table. One by one, they handed over their belongings and Lawson placed them in the bag. Christopher had wanted his toy lion, Kelly had given him a music box, and Thomas had trading cards, American football players in Lucite cases. John said the only things of value he had wouldn't fit, so he passed. Amy handed over a wrapped towel. Lawson opened it to reveal a matching brooch and necklace with sapphires. The brooch had been fashioned in the shape of a dragonfly.

"These have been in my family," Amy said.

"It's excellent work," Lawson said as he inspected the craftsmanship. "Have you ever had them appraised?"

"No," Amy said. "I'm pretty sure it's just costume jewelery."

Lawson rewrapped the towel, and once the jewelry was inside, cinched up the duffle. He placed it in the box. There was an abandoned gold mine nearby which could serve as the marker. After the sun had set, Lawson and Rainwood drove to the mine. Thomas had wanted to join them, but in the end was content to simply provide directions. Once they parked, they got out, measured a hundred-foot distance away from the mouth of the mine, and dug a hole. Lawson whistled the tune to "Nantucket Sleighride," by the band Mountain, as they worked. It had been a favorite of his when he was in country. The box buried, they filled the hole, covered it with debris, and returned to the ranch. Rainwood had drawn a map. He gave one copy to John and kept one for himself. They discussed what the next few days would look like with the family and said goodnight. Thomas had lingered for a moment. It seemed he was going to make another push to join them, but in the end thought better of it.

Rainwood and Lawson made some coffee. By now, the jetlag wasn't intolerable, but both men needed to be sharp, so they figured on staying up as late as they could. Outside, the temperature had dropped, though it was still humid. Had the mosquitos not been a problem, it would have been a perfect evening to stay on the porch. They reminisced about their old unit while they drank, and Rainwood took the opportunity to fill Lawson in on the history of the Rhodesian Bush War, or Second Chimurenga which was a Shona term for something like "revolutionary struggle." This was information Lawson hadn't been able to glean from his reading.

The conflict was similar to the war in Vietnam with numerous groups involved. Back there, it had been the North and the South, but it had bled into other countries like Cambodia. The same could be said for this conflict with countries that bordered Rhodesia like Mozambique. Most of the combat Lawson and Rainwood had seen in Vietnam was in the form of skirmishes with The Vietcong rather than The North Vietnamese Army. Here in Rhodesia, The Zimbabwe African National Union or ZANU, and its military force, The Zimbabwe African National Liberation Army or ZANLA, used hit and run tactics. That's who they'd been engaging. Rainwood finished his coffee and poured himself another cup.

Lawson didn't have a political stake in the game. Occasionally, while on patrol in Vietnam, their unit would find literature that had been left for them to find by The VC suggesting that US servicemen who were of minority descent were fighting the wrong war. Rainwood would remind them they were all there to execute the directive; that was it. If they began to contemplate what was right or wrong they would be opening a can of worms.

Here in Rhodesia, Rainwood had suggested they might run into some machine guns or perhaps a mortar attack, but it would be rudimentary. The problem would be similar to one they had already faced in Vietnam in that it would be almost impossible to be able to separate the enemy from friendlies.

As the hours crept along, they continued to catch up. Rainwood didn't elaborate much on what he'd been up to, but he filled in some of the gaps. It was mostly a struggle; he'd hit the bottle pretty hard, so a few months were lost to him forever, but he'd managed to rebound.

"And now, here we are," Rainwood said and gestured around the kitchen with his coffee cup. Lawson went into further depth about working for Seymour and how the guy had been ostracized by his community but had taken Lawson in as a favor and set him up as an apprentice. Eventually, Lawson would work his way up to a bench jeweler, but he was still wet behind the ears. Lawson had had nightmares for a while, but within the last few months those had begun to taper off. Lawson had been attending a support group with some other veterans, and he thought that was helping.

"Still taking action on anything with a pulse?" Rainwood said.

"The Pope Catholic?"

Lawson took his time savoring the memory of his latest triumph.

He made sure to recall every detail of his interaction with Fitzpatrick's bookmaking operation, including the peanut shells on the floor at Brennan's, and Sinatra on the jukebox. Horst had not been there on the day Lawson had come to collect when NC State won the basketball championship in March.

"How much did you win?" Rainwood said.

"A few grand."

"Herb."

"A little over fifteen large."

Rainwood laughed. It was the first time Lawson had heard Rainwood laugh in a long time. Rainwood stood and walked over to the kitchen. He came back a moment later with a bottle of brandy.

"Absolutely," Lawson said and lifted his cup.

Rainwood topped them both off, put the bottle back in the kitchen, then sat back down.

"Let me guess," Rainwood said. "You invested all the winnings in a mutual fund?"

"Close. Precious metals."

Both of them laughed. If there had been any tension from bringing up the past or addressing any potential problems moving forward, it had dissipated completely.

"I bet it all, and some more, on the Ali/Forman fight," Lawson said.

"All of it?"

"I put a few hundred toward living."

"Who'd you take?" Rainwood said.

"Foreman."

Lawson tried to gage what Rainwood was thinking but Rainwood's face gave nothing away.

"You remember what Foreman did to Frazier in Jamaica?" Lawson said.

Rainwood and Lawson had been in 'Nam at the time of the Foreman/Frazier fight, but both were fans of the sweet science, so they made sure to listen to the broadcast. The fight had taken place in Kingston, Jamaica, twelve hours behind them, so they'd catch it in the morning. As opposed to the NBA finals, Lawson didn't have to worry about catching hell for shirking his responsibility. Rainwood would clear them from whatever duties they had. Joe Frazier had been a gold medal winner in the '64 Olympics, and he was the current heavyweight champion. Frazier was undefeated and more importantly, had beaten Muhammad Ali by unanimous decision two years previously to lay a legitimate claim to the title.

Of course, Ali had been in exile for the previous few years, but that still didn't take anything away from what Frazier was able to accomplish. Foreman had also been a gold medalist in the '68 olympics, was similarly undefeated, and a good five inches taller than Frazier. Foreman also hit like a sledgehammer.

Had Lawson been listening to the broadcast with anyone else, he would have tried to get some action going, but Rainwood wasn't one for gambling. So, with nothing riding on the outcome, Lawson was simply content to listen to the results with Rainwood. The Frazier/Foreman fight didn't last very long. It only took two rounds for Foreman to beat Frazier. Foreman ended up knocking Frazier down six times en route to a stoppage.

"Did you get good odds on Foreman?" Rainwood said.

"Decent."

Rainwood nodded.

This was not the reaction Lawson had wanted, and it irked him. Lawson was not a professional handicapper by any stretch, but this result seemed like a slam dunk. Over the years, Lawson had met some people who'd spent all of their free time studying the intangibles, crunching numbers, or believing in omens before laying a bet.

There were no sure things, but he respected the odds. Granted, on paper, UCLA had looked like they should have won another championship, but they'd also won seven in a row and were due to be beaten.

Foreman was twenty-five, had destroyed Joe Frazier, and would reportedly leave dents in heavy bags he'd hit. Ali was thirty-two, had been inactive for three years of his prime, and lost to Frazier by decision.

"What do you know?" Lawson said.

Rainwood finished his coffee.

"Henri's seen Ali training."

"And?"

"That's it."

"He's seen him training?"

"Yeah. Ali looks ready."

Lawson knew he should have felt relieved that had been Rainwood's only evidence in backing Ali, but for some reason Lawson didn't feel relieved.

"What are—" Rainwood started to say but stopped when he heard the braying of one of the cattle. "Let's go," he said.

Immediately, both he and Lawson stood and grabbed rifles they had gotten from Henri. Earlier, Rainwood had asked the family about a translator, but Rainwood had been told most people spoke English. However, Thomas knew enough of the Shona language if they needed someone.

Rainwood knocked on Thomas's door. Within moments, Thomas had grabbed the repeating rifle and joined them.

Once they were outside Rainwood spoke. "Wait here," he said to Thomas.

Rainwood communicated the plan to Lawson using hand signals. Both men approached the cattle pen. There were five rustlers by the gate. Two of them had been working on the lock and three had been watching their comrades work. All had machetes with them. The three who'd been watching had rifles slung over their shoulders. None of these men had any training. Most likely, they had been students or farm hands, caught up in the mix, and here they were as irregulars rustling cattle.

Rainwood and Lawson got the drop on them.

"Don't move," Rainwood said in Shona. It was one of the few phrases he had made sure to learn.

All five men turned around. Had the three with the rifles had more seasoning, they might have tried something. However, all of them seemed to recognize Rainwood and Lawson were a cut above the previous security measures they'd been used to dealing with.

"English?" Rainwood said.

"Yes," one of the men said.

"All of you?"

"Yes," the man said.

"Thomas, we don't need you," Rainwood called out over his shoulder. Rainwood lowered his weapon and approached the men. They were young. Their clothes were torn and caked in dirt. Both Lawson and Rainwood had seen the look in the soldier's eyes before: the newly indoctrinated. If they survived the first few months, the look would disappear.

Rainwood approached the soldier who appeared to be the most defiant. Rainwood got within a few feet, quickly maneuvered the weapon, and hit the man in the face with the butt of the rifle. The soldier fell to his knees just after the sound of wood splintering suggested his nose was broken. One of the other soldiers, possibly a relative of the one who'd been hit, went for his weapon.

Rainwood shot the man in the chest, and he fell to the ground. None of the others moved. The soldier with the broken nose asked for help. The soldiers hesitated at first, but Rainwood had lowered his weapon, so they checked on their friend as he registered the pain of his broken nose and moaned on the ground. Lawson kept his weapon ready just in case, but he knew the attack had destroyed the soldier's resolve.

"Forget this farm," Rainwood said to the group and gestured with the weapon they could leave. Again, they hesitated, but once they realized he'd been serious about giving them an out, they gathered their wounded and dead comrades and fled.

Lawson and Rainwood watched them disappear and returned to the house. Thomas stood on the porch. Thomas had turned ashen, and the energy which had galvanized him was gone. The weapon which he hadn't put down since Lawson and Rainwood had arrived, now rested against the side of the house.

"Was that—?" Thomas trailed off and stared at the ground. Whether he was ashamed of himself for losing his impulse to participate or was just unable to deal with everything once it got real remained to be seen.

"They have to know we're serious," Rainwood said.

There was no ferocity in his delivery. He didn't rub the kid's face in it, but Thomas's desire to be directly involved in the fight was clearly gone.

"I'm going to go back inside," Thomas said. He made no effort to retrieve his weapon on his way back into the house.

By the second day, Rainwood and Lawson's jetlag had almost fully dissipated. By the third, they had developed a routine. The biggest threat proved to be boredom. The two men would walk the perimeter a few times a day. Rainwood would communicate with Henri through the radio Rainwood had procured. The family continued to take care of the responsibilities on the farm, and Amy tutored the three children. Lawson had offered to help out with statistics and probability, but that hadn't been necessary. He'd begun to bond more with Thomas after realizing the boy was a huge sports fan. Amy gladly took

Lawson up on helping tutor Thomas, but because he had been a dedicated student, Thomas didn't need it. Both Lawson and Thomas took it as an opportunity to talk about football, specifically Don Shula, who it turned out had been one of Thomas's heroes.

Lawson and Rainwood would walk the perimeter once in the morning, again after lunch, and one more time in the evening. Before dinner, Lawson would join Thomas while Rainwood would speak with Henri over the short-wave radio. Aside from setting them up with weapons, Henri also kept them updated with reliable intel.

Thomas's room looked like most teenagers' rooms, or so Lawson imagined. Furniture was sparse. There was a desk with a chair and a cabinet for a turntable with LPs. The kid had headphones that made him look like an aviator when he wore them. Most of his collection was British Invasion stuff, which fit, considering he could trace half of his roots back there.

The rest of the room was in essence a shrine to coach Don Shula, the former coach of the Baltimore Colts and current coach of the Miami Dolphins. Posters of Johnny Unitas, Jim Kiick, and Larry Czonka decorated the walls. Since Kiick and Czonka were known as "Butch Cassidy and The Sundance Kid," there was also a poster of that film depicting Robert Redford and Paul Newman attempting to shoot their way out of being cornered by Bolivian soldiers.

Lawson had seen the film when it first came out, but it had been a few years. Up close now, he studied the poster. Thomas had been sitting on the corner of the bed reading a copy of the most recent Ring Magazine. He looked up, noticed Lawson inspecting the film poster, and put the magazine down.

"Sort of like you and Rainwood," Thomas said. He pointed to the poster of Cassidy and Sundance.

"Hopefully not." Lawson laughed as it did not end well for them. "Anything good in there?" Lawson pointed toward the magazine.

The cover of the issue Thomas was reading depicted the busts of George Foreman and Muhammad Ali over a map of Africa. The fight was supposed to take place recently, but Foreman had injured himself during a sparring session. Rather than call off the bout, they pushed it back a month. The other festivities that had been planned— a music festival with James Brown, Bill Withers, B.B. King and more, went on as scheduled.

"Nothing you haven't already told me," Thomas said. "There is one thing, though."

Lawson took his usual spot at the desk and sat down. "What do you got?"

Thomas shifted to face Lawson, sat cross-legged with his elbows resting on his knees, and interlocked his fingers under his chin. He looked like a monk about to meditate or listen to the reading of scripture. "There's a rumor Mobutu rounded up a thousand known criminals and killed one hundred of them to make sure there's no trouble for the fight."

Lawson nodded. Sometimes he and Thomas went on philosophical tangents. Mobutu Sese Seko was the president of Zaire and ruled the country with an iron fist. It would make sense that to avoid an international incident, he would do whatever he could to dissuade insurgents from trying anything; even if it meant holding people without due process.

"Think that'll work?" Lawson said.

Thomas was going to answer, but hesitated. "It will," he said finally.

"But?" Lawson said.

"Well," Thomas began. "It's hardly a way to gain support?"

"True," Lawson said, then uttered, "Hearts and minds."

Thomas furrowed his brow. Lawson stood up as he often did when he was about to go off on a tangent. The length of these always changed, so Thomas made sure to get comfortable.

"If you handle things the way Mobutu has with Zaire, what kind of government is it?" Lawson said.

"A dictatorship."

"Sure, that, or totalitarian, despot; you get the idea. Now, ruling by fear can be effective, but there will always be tension. People will rebel. Even if they don't, how comfortable can you be if you're in power?"

Once again, Thomas began to formulate an answer before he realized it was a rhetorical question.

"Winning hearts and minds was a slogan used to get the support of the South Vietnamese during the late nineteen sixties."

Thomas sat up a little more. Lawson rarely spoke about Vietnam, so when he did, Thomas knew it was going to be important.

"However, you still need to understand the values of the people you're trying to help." Lawson went on to discuss the Strategic Hamlet Program in the early sixties which sought to provide a sustainable living environment while isolating the Vietnamese from Communist influence.

"The program failed for a few reasons. One reason was people had a powerful bond with their land due to ancestral ties. They didn't want to be moved," Lawson said. He went on to suggest more mistakes had been made by giving Roman Catholic refugees preferential treatment, and installing a Roman Catholic leader in South Vietnam. Lawson explained how Roman Catholicism represented a very small percentage of the population of Vietnamese. The Catholics among them had also been championed by the French, who had been the previous occupants in Vietnam.

"When was this?" Thomas said.

"In the early sixties. Before The US got involved in the fighting they had been advising." Lawson paused a moment.

"The US assumed they could have similar success in Vietnam as they had in the Philippines, but they didn't consider the differences between the two countries. The predominant religion in The Philippines is Catholicism. It's not in Vietnam."

Thomas sat in rapt attention. He opened his mouth once to speak, took a breath, and stopped. Lawson had come to understand that was Thomas's tell for when he wanted to ask a question but was hesitant to do so.

"You can ask me anything," Lawson said.

"Did you enjoy it?"

Lawson had his answer ready, but he paused. He wanted to make it seem like he'd never considered the question before and was coming up with the answer in the spur of the moment.

"No. I didn't enjoy it," Lawson said.

The truth was there had been aspects of it he enjoyed, but he didn't want to give the kid the wrong impression. Thomas nodded a few times and looked out his window. The room overlooked the cattle pen where they had braced the insurgents the previous evening.

"It's different when it's real, isn't it?" Thomas said aloud, though whether he had been speaking to Lawson was unclear.

Thomas turned his attention away from the cattle pen and back to Lawson. "Why do you do it?" he asked. This time there was no hesitation with the question.

"I owe Rainwood," Lawson said. He didn't need to consider the answer before revealing it. Whether the kid had wanted to know the details of his action in

Vietnam, how Lawson had been drafted for his first tour, reupped for a second, or spent five days in Pattaya in Thailand; the kid could wait for another time to hear all that. The truth was, outside of feeling obligated to help Rainwood, Lawson hadn't thought about it. Once the decision had been taken from him the first time, he just weighed the odds and made his choice. Even though he pretended otherwise, there hadn't been anything for him back home. Lawson checked the time. He and Rainwood needed to walk the perimeter one more time this evening and have their briefing.

"We can pick this up again tomorrow," Lawson said.

***

Rainwood had waited until after he and Lawson were sitting in the kitchen with their spiked coffees before he told Lawson the news he'd gathered from Henri.

"Retaliation?" Lawson said.

It turned out the rustler whose nose had been broken was a relative of a high ranking ZIPRA official. While originally, the ranch had been one of many targeted for rustling, they essentially had a bullseye on them now.

"What are the odds?" Rainwood said, lifted his mug, and took a healthy pull. He'd fixed his on the strong side, so he winced.

"Henri say when?" Lawson asked.

"Nothing definite, just something he picked up on the wire. Apparently, ZIPRA has bigger fish to fry at the moment, so my guess is it won't be for at least a few days."

Both men sat in silence for another minute, drinking, and contemplating the next move. Rainwood had also told Lawson that Henri had attended the music festival that was supposed to coincide with the Foreman/Ali bout, and though the crowd knew the boxing match was postponed, everyone still had a great time. The crowd could forget about everything for a few hours, and the performers put on a fantastic show. Henri hadn't divulged anymore about who might win the upcoming fight now that it was only delayed.

"How do you want to play it with the family?" Lawson said.

"We can give it to them straight."

"When?"

"No time like the present."

Both men made sure to fill their cups again and called for the family to join them in the dining room. It was practically a recreation of the meeting they had on the first day. Amy and John had taken the same positions as they had on the porch. Both seemed much more relaxed than they had previously, though.

Christopher was playing with a different toy this time: a train. He was still focused on the task at hand, and except for a rare moment when he grew disinterested, he was content to push the locomotive around in circles. Kelly may have in fact been wearing the exact same outfit she'd worn during their first meeting. She also seemed much more relaxed.

Thomas was the only one who appeared to have changed. He hadn't touched the Winchester since he'd left it leaning against the house the other night. The boy had never gone anywhere without the weapon, and now it gathered cobwebs in his closet. Though Lawson had assured Thomas he had nothing to feel ashamed about, the boy considered himself a coward and a failure.

Thomas hadn't said as much, but both Lawson and Rainwood could tell the fight had been driven from the boy. The family knew of the previous night's skirmish. They already understood the situation would be handled by Lawson and Rainwood using whatever measures both men thought acceptable. Rainwood informed them of the ramifications and the suspected retaliation.

"What are our options?" John said.

"What do you think we should do?" Amy said. Amy didn't emphasize the word you, but both Lawson and Rainwood got the sense she was deferring to their judgment.

"From the news I got, it sounded like this could be a serious threat," Rainwood said then added, "It might make sense for you to leave the country for a while."

"How Long?" Kelly said. It was the first time she'd spoken. In fact, Lawson couldn't remember the last time he'd even heard her voice. Aside from Thomas, who had undergone a radical change in disposition, Kelly had seemed remarkably stoic; however, Lawson surmised she was probably just very good at concealing how difficult these last few weeks and months had been for her. The tone in Kelly's voice suggested that the duress she'd been under was greater than Lawson or Rainwood had assumed. Even Christopher stopped playing with his toy for a moment. Whether the sound of his sister's voice seemed foreign to *him* remained to be seen. However, he quickly returned to pushing the train along the floor.

"I don't know," Rainwood began. "They might not even retaliate. Or, it might be a day to a month. We're prepared to go toe to toe with anyone, but there might be collateral damage."

"What do you think we should do?" Amy said again. This time she was a little more forceful. She wouldn't emasculate John outright, but once the safety of her children was involved, she got right to the point.

"I think you should leave the country," Rainwood said.

Rainwood and Lawson had briefly discussed it before the meeting, so they would be on the same page. Neither Lawson or Rainwood had a problem staying and duking it out with whatever force returned for retribution, but the family's involvement would complicate things. John, sensing this might be his opportunity to re-establish some control of the situation, spoke. "We could stay with my parents."

Amy nodded her head.

"I'd leave it open ended for now," Rainwood said. "Maybe a month." He looked to John, and added, "I think that's a good idea."

At the thought of going to England, Kelly's sullen disposition changed. Thomas still looked forlorn, and Christopher was oblivious.

"Take some time to sort out the details," Rainwood said.

It was Wednesday. Rainwood suggested they be ready to depart by the following Wednesday. They would need some time to book tickets back to England, but John's brother was a barrister with connections and could probably speed up the process. In the meantime, they would head South and stay at a hotel near The Jan Smuts international airport in South Africa. Once it had been agreed upon, the children returned to their rooms, but John and Amy stayed.

"What are you going to do?" John said to Rainwood.

"We'll stay here until you're out of harm's way," Rainwood said.

"And then you'll go?" Amy said.

"We'll make sure everything is handled."

It was a vague answer, but neither Amy or John prodded. Instead, they began discussing the various chores and arrangements they would have to make before they left. Rainwood and Lawson went outside to walk the perimeter.

"We probably won't be here for the fight," Lawson said. Whether they would have been able to travel to Zaire to take in the Foreman/Ali bout was a longshot, but Lawson would continue to speak about it as if it had been a real possibility.

"Sorry, Herb."

"It's all good," Lawson said.

When they finished walking the perimeter they returned to the house. Rainwood stayed outside and watched the sunset. Lawson had begun to make more of an effort to check in on Kelly. While they didn't have much to discuss, he could tell she appreciated his concern. This evening was brief as all of their encounters had been; each uttered a few words, and Lawson was on his way. Afterward, he went to Thomas's room for the weekly tutorial. Inside, Thomas had begun to remove some of the posters from his wall. His sullen demeanor still hadn't changed. He looked withdrawn and disillusioned. Jim Kiick, Larry Csonka, and Johnny Unitas were now rolled up on the bed. Butch Cassidy was in the process of coming down.

"You wanna do a modified session tonight?" Lawson said.

Thomas looked over his shoulder and went back to his work without saying anything.

"That's OK," Thomas finally said. He removed the other tack from the bottom, and the poster rolled up.

"I'm sure there's something—" Lawson began.

"It's fine, really."

Thomas hadn't looked back when he spoke. He'd continued to remove the rest of the tacks, rolled the poster up, and laid it on the bed next to the others. Lawson didn't say anything. Instead, he took out a piece of paper from his pocket and put it on the bed.

"This is the address of a jeweler I work for back in the world. If you ever need anything, you can write me there," Lawson said. He paused for a moment and added, "You're a good kid."

Neither spoke and Lawson took the opportunity to leave.

Lawson went to the room he shared with Rainwood who was laying on his cot listening to the radio. They had decided to move into the house after their skirmish with the rustlers, as Rainwood thought the family might become a target instead of the cattle.

It had been a spare room in the house the family had used for storage, but Lawson and Rainwood didn't need much. Within a half an hour, it had been turned into a suitable bedroom which was much better than some of the places they'd been. Whether or not the previous interaction with Thomas was apparent on Lawson's face, Rainwood turned down the radio to speak with him.

"You good?" Rainwood said.

"Fine," Lawson replied.

"OK."

Rainwood turned the volume back up. Lawson took a seat on his cot and the two of them listened to some classical music on one of the few international stations the radio got.

The next few days dragged on as the family made plans to return back to England. Walenti agreed to look after the ranch in the family's absence. John sold his cattle to another nearby rancher.

Otherwise, it was an uneventful time. Lawson and Rainwood stayed out of everyone's way as the family got ready for the journey. Both men continued to walk the perimeter a few times a day and solicited Henri for information. Henri hadn't heard anything new about a possible attack. Henri also kept them up to date with details of what he'd heard about either Foreman or Ali.

Finally, it was time for the family to leave. Each

member had already said their goodbyes to their friends. They had managed to secure to adjoining rooms at an airport hotel, and they'd be on a flight back to England the following week.

Rainwood and Lawson walked them out to a waiting car. Walenti would drive them to the hotel. Up close, Walenti had no defined musculature. However, Lawson had seen the man working around the ranch, carrying things which would have crippled both he or Rainwood had either of them tried to lift it, even if they had worked together.

Walenti helped gather the family's belongings. While he stowed the luggage, John and Amy took the final opportunity to discuss the plan with Rainwood and Lawson.

"We'll call you when we get to the hotel and again before we board the plane," John said.

"Sounds good," Rainwood began. "And we'll let you know when things have settled enough around here."

"About a month?" Amy said.

"It's difficult to tell, but I would say so."

"Thank you both," Amy said. John echoed her sentiments, shook hands, and the family got in the car. Lawson and Rainwood watched them drive off. Rainwood didn't linger. Lawson stayed until the car had fully disappeared from view. Thomas had still been a little standoffish, but Lawson hadn't held it against the boy. Lawson knew how he would have reacted when he'd been that age.

Thomas had Lawson's address back in the states; the kid knew how to get ahold of him. Lawson walked back inside. Rainwood was seated at the dining room table, which had now been converted to an armory. Weapons had been disassembled. Gun oil and rags were interspersed along with the various components. Rainwood was on the radio with Henri, and they were already in the middle of a conversation.

"That's right. The family just left. Put the word out me and Lawson are still here."

"Consider it done," Henri said. "Anything else?"

"It's been good working with you," Rainwood said.

"You as well my friend," Henri said followed by static.

Rainwood shut off the radio and went back to cleaning the weapons on the table. Lawson could tell Rainwood had started to get the itch that came before combat, so he didn't interrupt. Instead, he took a spot at the table and began loading bullets into excess clips. Henri had arranged for another delivery of firearms once Rainwood and Lawson had gotten settled.

Now that they had put out what had practically amounted to an invitation, they were glad to have the extra resources. Lawson finished loading the bullets, banged the clip against the table so the cartridges would be in alignment, and placed it next to a few others.

The next day or so shifted between boredom and anticipation. Depending on how fast word travelled, Henri might not be able to give them a heads up, so both Lawson and Rainwood would have to be prepared from here on out.

Now that it was just the two of them though, they fell back into the old rhythm of when they'd been in Vietnam. They set up defensive measures on the outskirts of the property: nothing that would provide a serious warning but would give them a few minutes to prepare for an upcoming engagement. Much of what they relied on were techniques they'd picked up from the Vietcong or other guerrilla forces.

They buried punji sticks: sharpened pieces of burned wood stuck in the ground, dug two deadfalls, and although they didn't have the time or aptitude to incorporate the subsequent weight intended to crush the victim, they figured the fall might cripple or at least delay the attack.

By the time they had finished, the sun had begun to dip. Both men returned inside for an evening drink. Lawson brewed the coffee and Rainwood cracked the seal on another bottle of whiskey. Once settled with mugs in their hands both men finally spoke. It had been over an hour since either had said anything.

"You going back to New York after this?" Rainwood said. His voice had an ethereal quality as though it would be the last time they would have the chance to speak like this.

"Yeah," Lawson said. "No need to keep chasing the dragon."

"What about after Foreman wins?" Rainwood said.

"I'm thinking maybe football next. I like Pittsburgh."

"The Steelers?"

"Just a feeling," Lawson said. "You?"

"We'll see."

They talked for another half an hour before they walked the perimeter for the final time and called it a night.

The assault came the next evening. One of the rudimentary traps Lawson and Rainwood constructed had worked, and the unfortunate soldier who'd tripped it screamed in pain. With the element of surprise now gone, the soldiers opened fire. They hadn't been as well trained or equipped as Lawson and Rainwood's former adversaries, the Vietcong, but once the bullets started flying it didn't matter. The ZIPRA troops maneuvered pretty effectively in the dark. They fired at the main ranch house and shot out the windows on one side. They tossed in a Molotov Cocktail which broke on the kitchen floor, and soon the entire room was engulfed as the fire spread.

Now that the family was gone, it was open season on the ranch.

Although the war had continued to escalate, the revolutionaries still probably wanted to avoid an international incident. It was one thing to rustle cattle or kill some mercenaries; it was another to lay waste to a family of expats. However, now the event would also act as a warning to other families in the area of what might happen if they chose to hire mercenaries.

Lawson and Rainwood had been in the barn when the soldiers attacked. The last two days, Lawson and Rainwood had split their time bivouacking outside or sleeping in the barn's loft. This evening, Lawson had been asleep with Rainwood on guard when the screaming started. It woke Lawson who'd always been a light sleeper, and within moments he and Rainwood were armed and ready. Initially, the ZIPRA soldiers had used the light of the moon to see what they were doing, but as the fire from the house continued to blaze, it lit up the night sky.

The family's pickup truck had been kept in the barn for work around the ranch. Rainwood and Lawson had previously checked the engine to make sure it would start, and now they would use it. It hadn't been suped up, but it had decent suspension and would serve their purpose. There looked to be a group of about ten ZIPRA soldiers, each armed with rifles and spread out in a formation to maximize the field of fire.

The plan would be to head out in the truck, strafe, and make another pass. Rainwood would drive, and Lawson would operate the Sanna 77— a machine gun they had gotten from Henri. There were forty rounds in a magazine. Lawson had kept one magazine inverted and taped it to the one that was inserted in the magazine well. When he was out of bullets, he'd just have to flip it over. The rest of the weapons, the radio, and enough food to last them away from the ranch for a few days had been stowed beneath the passenger seat in case they needed to abandon their post for an unforeseeable period.

Lawson climbed into the truck bed. He had created a harness by looping a belt through the back window and around the passenger seat head rest. Rainwood slid back the barn door and got behind the wheel. Normally, they would have been stealthier with their movements, but considering all eyes were on the ranch house, they figured they could be a little more cavalier. Rainwood turned the key in the ignition, the headlights shone, and they sped off. They still had the element of surprise. The truck burst forth from the barn and Lawson opened fire almost immediately. The soldiers had been expecting a counterattack from the house, not from the barn. A soldier who stood on the edge of the group absorbed the first few projectiles, and most of the others dropped where they stood or had begun to scatter. It happened so quickly only two of the soldiers managed to reset and open fire but were off target. Rainwood slowed and executed a 180 to make another pass. Lawson switched out clips.

On the next pass, Lawson managed to hit two more, but the soldiers who had reset were more accurate and some of their bullets pinged off the side of the truck. Rainwood continued driving until he had connected with the A6 highway. Rainwood and Lawson would regroup at one of the dams and return to the ranch the following day. Lawson kept an eye out for headlights, but he doubted they would be followed.

They reached the dam in about twenty minutes and Rainwood skidded to a stop underneath one of the sodium vapor lamps. Lawson hopped off the truck platform onto the ground. Even though there was enough light to see, he still used his flashlight. Lawson waited another moment and scanned the road for incoming vehicles, but there was nothing.

Lawson was full of adrenalin, but he knew he'd calm down in a few minutes. He walked toward the driver's side, shined his light, and noticed the bullet hole in the door. Inside, Rainwood's head rested against the steering wheel. Lawson frantically reached for the door handle, but it was locked. He banged on the window with his moonstick. Rainwood lifted his head, looked over, and blood began to turn his shirt maroon. Rainwood lifted the handle as Lawson opened the door. He tried to move and fell from the driver's seat into Lawson who quickly caught him.

"Jesus!" Lawson said.

He laid a semi-conscious Rainwood on the ground. Lawson didn't have any medical training, but he had been friendly with a combat medic who had filled him in on some basic techniques. Among the possessions Rainwood and Lawson had gotten from Henri were some morphine, bandages, and smelling salts. Lawson dove into the cab, found the kit, and was soon cracking the smelling salts under Rainwood's nose. Rainwood awoke with a gasp, and instantly the pain registered. Lawson injected Rainwood with a syrette of morphine, took the survival knife from his boot, and cut Rainwood's shirt open.

The tatters stuck to Rainwood's skin, but Lawson was able to push them aside. One of the bullets that had gone through the door of the truck hit Rainwood in the ribs. The bullet had not come out the other side, so it was probably still in Rainwood's chest cavity. This was way over Lawson's head, and he cursed aloud.

"That bad, huh?" Rainwood said.

Lawson could have begun a tirade telling Rainwood

he needed to hold on; he could load him back into the truck and drive to a hospital. Since they had only taken the A6 to get here, Lawson could find his way back to the ranch. The reality of the situation was he only had a vague idea of where the hospital was. Besides, he knew Rainwood had already lost a lot of blood. Essentially, he was already on borrowed time now.

"Well," Rainwood said. He lifted his hand, and Lawson took it.

"It's been worth it," Rainwood said.

"It has," Lawson said as his voice broke. Within a few moments, Rainwood had passed. Lawson picked Rainwood up and laid him in the truck bed. The man probably wouldn't have cared if he'd been left for the carrion, but there was no way Lawson was going to do that. He would wait another half an hour then drive back to the ranch. Once there, he'd bury Rainwood, contact Henri, and see about getting some sort of passage back home.

Lawson's mind raced as he drove, and he almost missed the turn off for the ranch. The enemy soldiers had dispersed, but Lawson wasn't going to leave anything to chance. Thankfully, the sun had begun to rise, so he didn't need to use his headlights. The frame of most of the house remained, but the rest of it was now a charred husk. A fire still burned, but it was slowly dying. Most of the belongings had been destroyed. Lawson parked the truck in front of the barn, went inside, and retrieved a shovel. He wouldn't erect a headstone, but at least he'd lay Rainwood to rest. He made certain to dig a deep enough hole, placed his friend's body inside, filled it back up, and said a few words.

Lawson took the radio from the truck. He didn't know what time it was, but the sun had risen.

"Henri," Lawson said into the handset. It took a few more attempts before Henri was roused.

"Yes," Henri said. He sounded as if he'd just awoken, so he was a little disjointed.

Lawson explained what had happened to Rainwood and requested a flight back to the United States as soon as possible. Henri had finally shaken the sleep from his voice, and when he answered, said there would be a transport plane leaving at the end of the week from South Africa. Lawson asked if there was anything sooner. Henri said there was another transport leaving from Kinsasha in forty-eight hours, if he could make it there by then. Lawson said he would. Over the next few minutes, Henri gave directions which Lawson committed to memory and repeated back. As they were finishing up, he heard vehicles approaching.

"I've got to go. I'll see you," Lawson said.

He turned off the radio before Henri could reply, grabbed a loaded rifle from the passenger seat, and watched as a lone car approached. The vehicle stopped about fifty feet away from Lawson and the truck. He had the weapon pointed in the general direction of the car, but wasn't aiming it. The passenger side opened, and the rustler from the other night with the broken nose stepped out.

"Where is your friend?" The solder said. He didn't have a weapon visible, but Lawson knew there were probably others close by.

"He's dead," Lawson said.

The man nodded a few times and spoke. "Then we are done." The man with the broken nose said, paused, then spoke again. "Go home. This is not your fight."

Lawson wanted to say he'd heard that before but instead simply said, "I will."

The soldier got back into the passenger seat and shut the door. Rather than go in reverse, the car continued forward to circle around Lawson and the truck. The car continued in a semi-circle until it pointed back toward the road. Lawson wasted no time. He paid his final respects to Rainwood, got in the truck, and started his drive. If he only stopped when necessary, he might make it in time.

———

Henri had been at the hotel bar near the airport in Kinshasa having a drink. When he had described himself to Lawson so they could find each other, he said he looked like an ancient philosopher. His description had turned out to be pretty accurate.

Henri had a Van Dyke beard and wild hair. His eyebrows were also unkempt which reminded Lawson of Groucho Marx. Lawson was exhausted and ran on fumes at this point, but he stayed with Henri for over a half an hour. They discussed the situation in Rhodesia, Rainwood, the family now in England, and ultimately the upcoming fight between Foreman and Ali.

Henri reiterated his stance on Ali, but at that point Lawson didn't have the strength to offer up a rebuttal. Henri drank red wine; Lawson went with coffee. The bar didn't have it, but they sent for it from the restaurant next door. Henri spent a good amount of time at the hotel as they were willing to appease him and his friend.

Lawson began to nod off, so Henri said he would drive Lawson to the airport, return to the hotel, and take care of the truck. Lawson asked about payment, what he had owed, but Henri said it wasn't necessary. Rainwood had given Henri a retainer which would take care of it. Finally, the two of them got into Henri's car and drove to the airport. Apparently, Henri had a few members of the airport staff on the payroll or had greased them well enough, so Lawson was able to bypass customs. As the plane was loaded, Lawson said his goodbyes to Henri. Before he climbed aboard, Lawson watched as Henri spoke to one of the crew who'd been loading the plane and handed the crewman an envelope.

Lawson found a seat, buckled in, and was asleep in no time.

Lawson managed to be under for more than half of the flight. His dreams were all nightmares involving Rainwood. In most of them, he'd have to drive his mortally wounded friend to the hospital, but they would either get stuck in traffic or the pedals and steering wheel would no longer respond to Lawson's commands. Somehow, Lawson knew that from now on the nightmares he'd learned to live with from Vietnam would be replaced by ones that focused on Rainwood.

As Lawson prepared to deplane at John F. Kennedy International Airport, the crew member who he'd seen speak with Henri back in Zaire waved him along. Lawson followed the crewman from the plane through some corridors. Along the way, they passed by a checkpoint where the crewman showed his identification and gave the envelope to security.

Lawson couldn't hear what the crewman said, but whatever it was had been enough and security waved them both through. He and Lawson continued walking for another minute until they got to a side door that led outside the terminal. The crewman gestured for Lawson to go.

"Thank you," Lawson said.

The crewman nodded. Lawson went outside. New York in the fall was a crap shoot, and this October had been cold. Lawson hadn't been prepared for it, so he began to shiver. He found a line for the taxi stand, and soon he was heading back to his apartment.

———————

"They've still got great blintzes."

Seymour had welcomed Lawson back with open arms, and though it had felt like a lifetime ago, by the second day back in the swing of things, Lawson had settled into a groove. Nothing had been upended in the few weeks he had been gone. The same wait staff worked the lunch rotation at the diner, Lawson could still do the work required of him, and as many times as he said he could, Seymour still turned down the offer to bring back something from the diner.

It felt good to be home.

Rainwood still haunted Lawson at every conceivable moment, but Lawson knew the hold Rainwood's memory had would weaken over time. The trick was to avoid getting hooked on something like booze or drugs to try and dull the pain. It would be difficult, but it could be done.

The first two weeks he was back, he made a concerted effort to reconnect with his old unit; first, to let them know about Rainwood, but he had also wanted to do a better job of staying in touch. Jackson hadn't been able to post bail, and Raskavanitch was still MIA. Lawson was able to speak with parents of both, who thanked Lawson for calling and said they would relay the message about Sergeant Rainwood.

Lawson was able to get a hold of Dom Garibaldi, and the two of them caught up for about a half an hour. Lawson waited until the end to reveal Rainwood's fate, and Garibaldi seemed to take it well, but Lawson knew it would eat at the man just as it did to Lawson.

Garibaldi thanked Lawson for calling, said they should both speak again soon, and hung up.

Most importantly, Lawson tried to spend as much time as possible with Seymour who had been happy to have Lawson's company. Seymour would invite Lawson into his office and they would usually have a drink after work. While Seymour never asked what had happened in Africa, Lawson volunteered the information. He left out certain details, but eventually, he'd told Seymour the entire story. Seymour had been empathetic and provided as much solace as he could. Lawson was grateful for the opportunity to speak about it. Seymour also opened up about his own family, and the decision he made to marry the woman he loved despite what it had cost him. While many of the subjects were morose or serious, Seymour and Lawson also talked sports.

The date of the Foreman/Ali fight was finally here. Seymour wasn't a fan of boxing, but growing up he had worshipped "Hammering" Hank Greenberg, the baseball player. Although, The Giants, Dodgers, or Yankees would have been suitable for most kids who'd grown up in one of the five boroughs in New York, Seymour was a fan of The Detroit Tigers since that was Greenberg's team. Except for a single season Greenberg had played for Pittsburgh, Hank Greenberg had been in Detroit.

That night, Seymour and Lawson spent another hour together reliving Seymour's memories of game 5 of the 1945 World Series between the Chicago Cubs and the Detroit Tigers.

"It was Sunday, so we could listen to the game on the radio," Seymour began. He went on to say his parents hadn't been interested in the baseball game, although they appreciated there was an observant Jewish player for whom their children could follow.

"The series had been tied two games apiece," Seymour said and took a sip of his drink. The World Series that year had been a rematch of Chicago and Detroit from ten years previously. Hearing Seymour talk about Chicago reminded Lawson of Raskavanitch.

Seymour didn't recount each inning pitch by pitch, or anything like that, but there had been some memorable moments he said he would never forget. Hank Greenberg, who'd just been discharged from military service came through for them by hitting the only two home runs Detroit would have during the series. Seymour, Seymour's brother, and two of their cousins sat captivated by the radio announcer's description of the game.

"At the time, there was nothing more important," Seymour said.

Whether or not it was a conscious gesture, Seymour glanced at the photo of his wife and children on his desk.

"Hank Greenberg meant everything to me and Schmuel. Listening to his exploits on the radio..." Seymour trailed off. Schmuel was Seymour's older brother. At the time of the '45 World Series, they would have been in their early teens. Lawson didn't know Seymour's age, but he pegged him somewhere around forty.

"Was it worth it?" Lawson said.

Seymour was about to go off on another tangent about Hank Greenberg's exploits but stopped. It took him a moment to realize that Lawson had been speaking about Seymour's wife and child. When Seymour understood, his face became sullen.

Lawson regretted asking the question almost as soon as he said it.

"Sorry," Lawson said.

Seymour put up his hand and motioned that it was fine to ask. Lawson couldn't help but compare the scene to his own sessions with Thomas only a few weeks ago.

"There have been good times," Seymour began and picked up the framed photograph of his wife and kids. "There have been bad times. But I don't regret my decision."

Lawson had heard from colleagues about some of the details of Seymour's choice to marry outside of his faith and what it ultimately meant. Seymour would be shunned by his family and friends, all those who'd he'd grown up with. Lawson knew he'd never be able to fathom the depth of what Seymour had gone through.

Seymour noticed the time and said he needed to get going. Lawson said he'd lock up for the evening.

"By the way, I almost forgot. A letter came for you, boychik."

Seymour picked up an envelope from a stack on his desk and handed it to Lawson. It was an international letter with a British address.

"Thank you, for everything," Lawson said.

Seymour collected his hat and coat, thanked Lawson for the trip down memory lane, and wished him a good evening. Lawson poured himself one more and sat at Seymour's desk.

He opened the letter. It was from Thomas. Thomas began the letter suggesting that though he might never receive a response from Lawson, Thomas would send his letter anyway, and hopefully it would allow him to express some of his regret. Thomas apologized for being so distant right before the family left, and wanted Lawson to know he truly had appreciated the time they spent together.

The rest of the letter explained how the family had been coping with the transition back to England. Everyone was making the best of the situation. Kelly had taken to everything pretty quickly. Thomas's grandparents had been generous, so it took a lot of pressure off of John and Amy who were both continuing to settle. Thomas ended by saying he wished both Lawson and Rainwood well.

The boxing match was going to air tomorrow night. It would be 4:30 am in Kinshasa, so it could be prime time in the US. Lawson spun around in his chair and let his mind drift; he thought about where he might watch the fight and what he might include in his letter back to Thomas. He did a doubletake when he saw the dragonfly brooch and matching necklace on the spine of one of Seymour's books.

Lawson ripped the book from its spot on the shelf and scanned the table of contents. His heartbeat elevated, and he reminded himself the odds were not in his favor. He quickly flipped to the corresponding pages. There it was: the dragonfly brooch.

Again, Lawson reminded himself of the chances. He scanned the description. There was something about the fabrication being for French nobility as well as the circumstances surrounding its disappearance and theories as to who might have stolen it. Lawson found the specifications and quickly read them.

He remembered noticing a flaw while he examined Amy's jewelry before putting it the lock box. Now, As Lawson read about the brooch, he held his breath. Upon discovering the brooch had the same flaw, he exhaled loudly, and let loose a string of profanity. He copied down the information, along with contact information for a few British jewelers Seymour had done business with in the past, put the book back, and locked up the office.

On his way home, a plan began to form.

———

By the beginning of round 7, Muhammad Ali was decisively winning the fight again George Foreman. It hadn't been open scoring, but it was pretty clear Ali had won the majority of the rounds. Lawson had kept the fight on in the background while he packed his belongings.

The fight no longer had the same hold over him. The odds on the fight had dropped to 4 - 1 in favor of Foreman just before the bell rang. Foreman winning would still ensure a huge payout for Lawson, yet since he'd read about the brooch, he'd been able to think of little else.

Lawson had been able to get a flight back to Rhodesia and would be there for less than a week. He'd already made inquiries through some connections made through Seymour and lined up a fence for after he'd acquired the goods.

Round 8 began as Lawson continued to pack his suitcase, but he stopped to watch. By now, Ali's game plan had become clear. He was hoping Foreman would tire himself out. Ali would lay on the ropes, absorb punishment, and when Foreman slowed, Ali would counter.

Foreman's swollen face displayed the results of Ali's work.

With about 20 seconds in the round, Ali, who had been playing possum, caught Foreman with a series of right hands. Ali sent Foreman to the canvas with about 10 seconds left in round 8.

Now, Lawson felt the first twinge of panic. He was surprised he hadn't felt it through 7 rounds, but seeing Foreman on the canvas had brought on the first wave. As the fear began to snowball, the referee continued the count. Foreman began to rise with around 2 seconds, but wobbled and fell back to the canvas. As Foreman went down, Ali held back delivering another blow. It was as if Ali didn't want to disturb the picturesque moment.

Muhammad Ali had won the fight with an 8th round knock-out.

"Oh, shit," Lawson said.

Lawson sat down and put his head in his hands. He'd had some losses before, sure, who hadn't? But this one was different. Lawson didn't have the balance to cover the loss, and Fitzpatrick would want his money ASAP. Lawson could pay the balance after he'd found the jewelry. He just needed to buy some time. Lawson picked up the phone and dialed the number for the bar. Fitzpatrick wouldn't leave the table, but Lawson could speak to Ridley. The guy might be a number cruncher, but he seemed reasonable.

"Brennan's."

"Yeah, Ridley there?"

"One sec. Who's this?"

"It's Herb Lawson."

Lawson could hear the sounds of the bar in the background as well as Frank Sinatra. In a minute, Ridley was on the phone. "Yes?"

Ridley could have opened with a pithy comment about the result of the fight, but that wasn't his style. He may have been socially awkward, but was all about business. Lawson had rehearsed what he was going to say, and he wanted to keep it short. He explained how he just needed until next week to cover part of what he owed. Going into further details would only serve to undermine his good will.

"Can you guarantee me an extension with Mr. Fitzpatrick?"

"I can't guarantee it, but I'll bring it up to him."

"Thank you."

Lawson hung up.

There was nothing else to be done. Lawson still felt

apprehensive, but he'd deal with the obstacles as they presented themselves. Hopefully, Ridley would be able to buy Lawson some time. Lawson continued to pack. He figured in case Ridley wasn't able to pull some strings, he'd stay somewhere else until the flight's departure.

Lawson would also call Seymour and let him know about him having to miss work for a few days. After Lawson had fenced the merchandise, he would be able to pay off Fitzpatrick. While he had probably burned that bridge in terms of placing more bets, there were other bookies out there.

About twenty minutes had gone by since Lawson's call to Ridley, and he only had a few more errands before hitting the road. He called Seymour and explained he had to leave town for a few days. Lawson had accrued enough sick time, so this wasn't like when he'd disappeared before. Seymour, as understanding as he always was, said it wouldn't be a problem. Lawson hung up the phone, shut off the TV and lights, grabbed his bag, and went outside into the hallway. He shut and locked the door behind him.

"This just ain't your night," a voice said.

Lawson turned and saw Horst resting against the wall about thirty feet away.

"Been there long?" Lawson said.

"Just after Ridley spoke to Fitzy, who gave the go ahead to come see you. So, five minutes?" Horst said.

"Gotcha."

Lawson straightened up a little. The adrenalin had begun to discharge as it had so many times previously.

"I figured you'd try to run," Horst said and gestured toward Lawson's luggage. Lawson could have taken the time to explain himself, but he knew it wouldn't matter.

"Aren't you even going to ask me if I have the money?" Lawson said.

"We still playing that game?" Horst walked forward. He wasn't holding any weapons.

"You sure you want to do this?" Lawson said.

Horst stopped. "You have no idea how long I've been waiting for this." He resumed closing the distance between them and was now fifteen feet away.

Lawson had left most of the weapons with Henri before he returned to the states. However, he'd forgotten to give Henri back the Browning Hi Power. When Lawson had arrived home, the weapon was still in his duffle bag. He purchased a holster for it, and since he was possibly going to be in the crosshairs again, thought he'd wear it.

As Horst approached, Lawson opened his coat and removed the Browning. Horst's eyes went wide as the first two shots took him in the chest. He fell backward onto the hallway floor. The sound of the weapon firing rendered Lawson deaf for a moment. As Horst squirmed around and bled out, Lawson walked over and put one in Horst's head.

In a moment, sound had started to return and the smoke from the gun barrel dissipated, but Lawson was already moving. He grabbed his bag and bolted down the stairs. As he descended to the lobby, he heard the beginnings of a conversation in which one of his neighbors had opened their door and seen Horst's body, then told her husband to call 911.

Outside, Lawson hailed a cab. He couldn't think of a place to go except Seymour's office. Lawson gave the driver the address, and the car pulled into traffic. Lawson tried to think of anything he might be missing that he'd need to deal with immediately. He ran through the steps of what he assumed would happen.

The police would ID Horst, who most certainly had a record. Once they had identified Horst, the detectives would speak with Fitzpatrick, a known associate, who would certainly give up Lawson. Lawson would become a person of interest sought for questioning, but by that time Lawson would be out of the country.

Odds were, Lawson wouldn't be able to return to New York for a while, if at all. Either way, that was a problem for the future. Lawson just needed to make it through the next few hours. He would go to the office, call Seymour, and head to the airport.

Once inside the office, Lawson sat down at Seymour's desk. He called information and spoke to a helpful person who gave him Seymour's number. Lawson dialed the number and stared at the photograph of Seymour and his family as the phone rang. Seymour picked up after the fourth ring.

"Hello?"

"Seymour it's Herb Lawson. Sorry to call you so late."

Lawson heard Seymour's wife ask if everything was OK.

"It's fine, Thelma," Seymour said. "Give me a second."

Lawson heard Seymour explain he was going to take the call in the den, so Thelma could go back to sleep. Seymour would go to the den and let her know when she could hang up the phone. A few moments went by, and Seymour said he was ready. Lawson waited until Thelma hung up the phone before he spoke.

"I'm in trouble," Lawson said.

"Start at the beginning," Seymour said.

Lawson went through the story. Lawson had already told Seymour about his gambling habit during one or more of their many evenings together having a drink after work. So, he quickly caught Seymour up with the particulars of his current situation that began with picking Foreman to win, Ali winning the fight, Lawson calling to get an extension on his debt, and Horst, Fitzpatrick's enforcer, finally coming to collect.

Lawson left out some of the details like finishing off Horst when he was down, but he also didn't make it seem like it had strictly been self-defense. Lawson didn't know why, but for some reason it was important to be transparent with Seymour.

"How can I help?" Seymour said.

"I'm going to have to leave town for a while. I don't know when I'll be able to come back."

Seymour didn't speak, but Lawson could hear him breathing. Eventually, he responded. "Do what you have to do."

"The cops will probably want to speak to you," Lawson said.

"Don't worry, Boychik. I haven't seen you."

"Thank you."

"Where are you?" Seymour asked.

"At the office," Lawson said.

"Good. There should be a folder with two hundred dollars in the top drawer of my desk. Take it."

Lawson opened the drawer and found the folder. He felt a mix of emotions, but confusion seemed to be the most powerful at that moment.

"Why—" Lawson began to say but trailed off. As if Seymour could read Lawson's mind, he answered the question. "It's called Tzedakah; an obligation to help."

There was a pause, then Lawson spoke. "Thank you."

"You're welcome," Seymour said. "Stay in touch."

Having to conduct business around the world meant Seymour's office had been set up to make international calls. Lawson had remembered the name of the hotel and bar Henri said he frequented, and now Lawson was rolling the dice in the hope Henri had not been exaggerating how often he spent time there. It took a few minutes of being transferred from operators to hotel staff, but eventually the bartender got Henri on the phone. Lawson kept the urgency of the situation from him but did mention how he would be returning to Rhodesia immediately to retrieve something valuable he had left behind. Lawson wouldn't be able to give Henri an advance, but he would gladly pay him afterward. This time, aside from weapons, Lawson would also need a guide to accompany him on his journey. Henri listened and waited until Lawson had finished providing the details. He agreed to the terms and told Lawson how everything would transpire once he arrived in the country. While the situation in Rhodesia wasn't optimal, nothing had escalated too much in Lawson's absence. He told Henri he would be flying into the Nkomo Airport.

"Go to the Bulawayo Lodge hotel; it's near the airport, and ask the concierge to put you in touch with Rufaro," Henri said.

Lawson wrote down the name. "Thank you, Henri."

"No problem. I'll take care of everything else."

They both hung up the phone. Lawson took his time wiping down Seymour's office. He wasn't so much concerned for himself, but he didn't want to implicate Seymour in anything should the cops investigate the office.

When Lawson was finished, he hailed a cab to the airport. Odds were, police had been notified of Horst's death and were on the scene canvassing Lawson's apartment complex and speaking to any witnesses. Except for the neighbor who called 911, there probably wouldn't be anyone for the detectives to question. It would take time to ID Horst's body and come up with a list of people. By that time, Lawson would be in the wind. He could worry about his return to New York City later. In the meantime, he began to devise a plan for how he would retrieve the jewelry and ultimately, how he would fence the goods once he'd procured them. He'd also taken a list of names from Seymour's rolodex.

Lawson didn't have any trouble at Kennedy International Airport, and while it was slow going, he made it through customs without any hold ups. This time, since it wasn't a transport plane, he'd have a layover in Johannesburg, before finally touching down in Bulawayo, Rhodesia. There would be plenty of time for Lawson to consider all of his options and figure out what moves he could make in the future. Lawson put on his complementary headphones and zoned out while listening to a classical station. He didn't imagine being able to sleep so easily, but by now the adrenalin in his system was gone, and he was out cold for the duration.

Lawson had another dream about being unable to help Rainwood, but this time it was connected to a scene in which he had also killed Horst. Lawson had been arrested, stood trial, and had to answer for both men's deaths. He awoke from the dream before he could be sentenced by the judge.

Once Lawson had arrived in Bulawayo, he caught a second wind. He had been able to exchange the bulk of the money Seymour had given him while still at JFK. He got a better exchange rate than he would have if he'd exchanged money at his destination, and while he didn't necessarily subscribe to it, Lawson took that as a good omen. He hailed a cab from the airport and checked into the Bulawayo lodge. Even though there was still fighting on the front, it had not reached the airport or the hotel. There had been some traffic, but it was just the typical congestion.

The concierge at the lodge was a middle-aged man whose skin sagged as if he'd been obese and had lost too much weight too quickly. The concierge had salt and pepper hair that was kept in a crew cut, and the suit he wore was one or two sizes too big. Lawson noticed the man was missing fingers from his hand. He paid for a room, told the concierge he was expecting a visit or call from a Mr. Rufaro, and made sure to include a generous tip. The concierge assured him no one had solicited Mr. Lawson, but would take care of everything as soon as Mr. Rufaro made contact.

Lawson took the key for his room, thanked the concierge, and suggested that he would be next door at the restaurant; Rufaro could meet him there. The concierge nodded again and confirmed he would make sure everything went smoothly. Lawson dropped his luggage in his room, went next door, and got a table. He ordered some coffee and was still looking over the menu when a woman sat down at his table.

"Mr. Lawson?" she said.

"Yes." He put the menu down.

"I am Rufaro."

Even though he had eaten on the flight, Lawson ordered food. While in basic training, he had learned you always eat when you can. Rufaro just had some iced tea. They spent the next fifteen minutes or so regaling each other with some of their experiences. Lawson spoke about his tours in Vietnam and his more recent exploits with Rainwood there in Rhodesia. He also suggested he'd left something valuable behind and needed to retrieve it, but those were all the details he divulged. Lawson didn't know how much Henri had already told Rufaro, but Lawson figured he'd play it close to the vest for now.

Rufaro had lived in Shurugwi with her husband, Faraji, and their children. Shurugwi was a small town about 200 kilometers away from Bulawayo. Faraji had been a member of the British South African Police force: specifically, the PATU, which was the Police Anti-Terrorist Unit, a paramilitary arm responsible for engaging with guerrillas. It was how Faraji had met Henri. Faraji would moonlight for Henri as a fixer. Over time, Henri had practically become a member of the family. The PATU consisted of small teams of five known as "sticks." The lead would always be a black policeman who could liaise and act as an interpreter. Faraji had been the lead officer of his stick. One evening, he and his team had provided backup for a unit that was going to investigate a report of illegal activity at an abandoned gold mine.

"A gang had taken up there since it was easy to defend, and they could mine for gold deposits." Rufaro stopped and took another sip of her drink. Her eyes had begun to well, and she needed a moment to regroup. "The gang favored using machetes."

Lawson nodded. He steered the conversation toward the task at hand. His food arrived and he gave her some of the details while he ate. She asked a question or two when it was relevant to the mission, but otherwise she let him speak. Lawson finished his meal and paid the bill.

Rufaro's car was parked just in front of the restaurant. Once seated inside, she gave Lawson a map so he could navigate, as well as a fully loaded Colt M1911.

"Thank you," Lawson said. He could still smell the oil— a sign it had recently been cleaned.

"The rest of what you asked for is in the back seat," Rufaro said.

"Great."

"Where are we going?"

Lawson gave her the address and told her he could guide her once they got on the highway.

"I need to visit an old friend," Lawson said as they pulled out of the parking lot.

The ranch house was no longer there, and the barn had been razed. Rufaro said the area would most likely go to the current administration, or if the opposition won, they would seize the land for redistribution. It was difficult to predict. Although, the longer the conflict went on, the more it favored the insurgents.

Now, Lawson and Rufaro stood on open plains while Lawson tried in vain to find his former comrade. As much as he searched, though, Lawson couldn't be certain of Rainwood's final resting place.

"This is what I get for not leaving a headstone," he said.

"I'm sorry?"

"Nothing, I'm just— speaking to myself."

She nodded as if she understood, and again Lawson tried to get his bearings. He counted the paces from where he imagined the front door of the house had been. He figured that would be as good a place as any, and more importantly, Rainwood would have understood. Lawson would have felt foolish if he had said anything out loud, so he was content to memorialize Rainwood in his mind. Every so often he would scan the view of the plains surrounding him and be reminded of conversations he and Rainwood had had while walking the perimeter. The sun was beginning to set, so Lawson made a final show of respect and indicated he and Rufaro could leave.

Once inside the car, Rufaro spoke. "Who was it?"

She gestured toward the ground near where Lawson had stood. There was genuine concern in the tone of her voice; Lawson got the sense she had known a lot of people who had died before their time, but her reaction hadn't been blunted.

"A former mentor," Lawson said, and she seemed to accept that as a suitable answer.

"Where next?" She asked.

Lawson looked at the map and gave her directions to the mine.

It was dark out by the time they arrived, but there were still dim lights that illuminated the opening. Lawson hoped he'd have more luck remembering the location of the box, but at this point he wasn't too concerned. He would find it.

"OK," Lawson said. He reached into the back seat, grabbed the entrenching tool and a lantern. "I'll be back soon, just watch my 6."

"Pardon?" she said.

"Sorry; please watch my back."

She nodded, and he exited the car. He walked to the mine's entrance, turned, and began humming the tune to *Nantucket Sleighride*. He was hoping somehow the memory of the exact location would return, but it hadn't. He just remembered one hundred paces. So, he might have to dig a few holes. Lawson lit the lantern and started moving.

"*Goodbye, little Robin Marie. Don't try following me,*"

Lawson sang as he walked. He counted a hundred paces, placed the lantern down a few feet away, and started digging. In the distance, Rufaro had turned off the headlights, so Lawson could barely make out the outline of the car, but he could still see it. It was reassuring to know she was there.

Except for the light from the lantern and the opening of the mine, it was pitch black out. The wind had picked up a little, and the weather had grown colder. In the distance, Lawson could hear the sounds of the plains picking up as animals communicated with each other.

He touched the butt of his weapon absentmindedly after the first sound, then calmed down and realized it was just white noise. He continued to dig until he'd gone about six inches, stopped, and started another hole. He struck the box on the fourth hole.

Lawson gave a thumbs up sign to Rufaro.

He had to assume she'd seen him, but she didn't honk or shine the lights, so he couldn't be certain. He spent the next minute clearing the debris and prying the box from the earth.

"Ndiwe ani? Uri kuitei pano?" a voice said from behind him.

Lawson turned to see four men standing fifteen feet away between him and the mouth of the mine. They all wore soiled clothes that looked like they hadn't been washed in weeks. Each carried machetes. Lawson didn't answer. If he went for his piece, he'd be cut down. These men all looked like they were familiar with bloodshed and needed little provocation. Lawson was about to speak when gunshots broke the silence. The four men were cut down by machine gun fire.

A moment later, Rufaro emerged from the darkness carrying a Bren light machine gun, the barrel smoking. She stopped walking. While she was still far enough away from Lawson, she opened fire again on the bodies. Rufaro continued to fire until the clip had emptied. The look on her face was one Lawson had not seen since he'd been in country. Rufaro seemed to be entranced; once the weapon dry fired a few more times, she stopped, looked at Lawson, and spoke.

"Are you ready?"

"Yes," Lawson said but hadn't begun to move. She stared at him for a moment.

"Right." He opened the box, removed the duffle, and slung it over his shoulder. He took the piece from his waistband, picked up the lantern, and started towards the car.

"Wait," she said and walked toward the bodies. Lawson stopped and watched her approach. A canvas bag was on the ground next to the dead men. Rufaro picked it up. One of them, who had been acting dead, slid a body off of him, sat up, and swung his machete.

Lawson shot the man twice: once in the elbow and the next in the head. The man had dropped the machete before it could make contact with Rufaro, though she was in range for the blood spatter which followed. She didn't scream or react, yet another sign that she'd probably seen much worse up close. Bag in hand, she followed Lawson to the car.

Rufaro drove. Once on the highway, Lawson inspected the contents of the duffle. Everything was still there and undisturbed. Rufaro had put the bag she'd taken and the Bren in the trunk.

"What was in the bag?" Lawson said.

"Gold," she replied.

Lawson sipped the remnants of his coffee as the plane began its descent into London Heathrow Airport.

Lawson stayed at the Bolewayo lodge for another week and had finally allowed himself to decompress from the cacophony of the previous few days.

Rufaro had taken the gold and gone to split it with Henri. When they later spoke, Henri told Lawson the gold was about a kilogram, which meant he could probably get about $6000 for it. Lawson suggested Henri and Rufaro split the entire sum, and while Lawson still offered Henri a piece of what he was hoping to get from the fenced merchandise, Henri declined. The gold alone would suffice. Plus, Henri had been thinking of retiring one of these days. He could hand the business over to Rufaro who had shown keen ability and would make a great addition to the operation.

Lawson broke from the memory. He took the bag from underneath the seat in front of him and examined the contents. He opened the case he'd bought to house the jewels to make sure they were still there. There was no reason to assume they wouldn't be, but it was a nervous habit. Lawson didn't remove the brooch or the necklace, but once he was satisfied they were still there, he shut the case and placed it back in the bag.

While almost all of Seymour's business was conducted above board, Seymour did have contacts throughout the world who were more unscrupulous with their business practices. Martin Festinger happened to be one of those people. Festinger lived just outside of London and though he didn't operate exclusively in the jewelry business, he knew enough people who would be interested in rare items such as the ones Lawson was looking to sell.

At one point, Lawson had considered contacting the proper authorities and returning the jewelry. Perhaps there would be a reward. However, the more he thought about it, the more he realized it would ultimately be a can of worms. In the end, Lawson had no problems contacting Festinger, who, once Festinger had vetted Lawson, would be more than happy to act as an intermediary.

Lawson didn't know who his counterpart would be in the transaction. To avoid walking into a trap, Henri had also given Lawson the names of a few people who could look out for his safety while he conducted business. Lawson had made plans to rendezvous with a former British SAS operative who was handy with a sniper rifle.

Lawson continued to rummage around the bag until he felt the Lucite cases containing the trading cards. He also felt the outlines of the toy lion and the music box. He took out the Lucite cases of the various athletes to make sure they were all there, shut the bag, and placed it back under the seat.

During one of the phone calls with Festinger, Lawson had been told the counterparty would be happy to offer 100,000 pounds for the brooch and necklace provided it proved legitimate. Lawson was able to talk the counterparty up to 125,000. Festinger assured Lawson that would be doable. They were able to set up a time and place to meet and conduct business. It would be Lawson, Festinger, the counterparty, the counterparty's security detail, and a jeweler who could verify the contents of the merchandise. Lawson would also have his SAS backup stationed nearby. He allowed for the counterparty to dictate the terms; except for the fact that Lawson wanted the meeting to happen outside. That was Lawson's only demand, and he was assured that would be fine. The rest of the details were ironed out, and the meeting was set to take place in two days.

The pilot came over the intercom telling the passengers they'd be touching down in about ten minutes and gave last minute instructions to be executed by the flight crew. Lawson finished his coffee and threw the cup away when one of the flight attendants came by with the trash bag.

Lawson had been focused on making sure the deal with the jewelry went smoothly and hadn't thought much about what he would do after the transaction had been completed. 50,000 of the money would go to Seymour; it was the least Lawson could do considering how much Seymour had helped him over the last few years.

Lawson had left a coded message for Seymour saying that his mission in Rhodesia was successful and they would be in touch. However, he didn't know whether the investigation into Horst's demise was still ongoing, and whether he had been implicated or not. Lawson would get a hold of Seymour soon and find out whether he would be able to return to New York. If it was possible, he would give Seymour the money then. If not, he would make sure to wire it.

Lawson would give 60,000 to John and Amy's family. He would also return the rest of the items to the children. While he hadn't necessarily thought about the reunion, Lawson realized he was truly looking forward to seeing everyone and would especially enjoy catching up with Thomas.

Lawson figured he'd keep 15,000 for himself. It would be a suitable amount for him to get acclimated wherever he decided to end up. Plus, he'd have some money to gamble with.

ABOUT THE AUTHOR

Andrew Davie has worked in theater, finance, and education. He taught English in Macau on a Fulbright Grant, at the university level in New York and Hong Kong, and at the middle/high school level in Virginia. Currently, he's pursuing his Clinical Mental Health Counseling Degree, and has survived a ruptured brain aneurysm and subarachnoid hemorrhage.

He has published short stories in various places, a memoir and addendum, and crime fiction books with All Due Respect, Close to the Bone, Alien Buddha Press, and Next Chapter. He also co-hosts a music review show called Happy Hour with Heather and Guest.

To learn more about Andrew Davie and discover more Next Chapter authors, visit our website at www.nextchapter.pub.

Range
ISBN: 978-4-82415-363-0
Mass Market

Published by
Next Chapter
2-5-6 SANNO
SANNO BRIDGE
143-0023 Ota-Ku, Tokyo
+818035793528

12th October 2022

www.ingramcontent.com/pod-product-compliance
Lightning Source LLC
LaVergne TN
LVHW031240190726
843491LV00012B/3066